who Found Easter

By CHARLOTTE ZOLOTOW

Illustrated by BETTY PETERSON

A TRUMPET CLUB SPECIAL EDITION

To Steve, who gave me the idea

ISBN 0-590-30024-5

Text copyright © 1959 by Charlotte Zolotow. Text copyright © renewed 1987 by Charlotte Zolotow. Illustrations copyright © 1959 by Betty Peterson. Illustrations copyright © renewed 1987 by Betty Ferguson. All rights reserved. Published by Scholastic Inc., 555 Broadway, New York, NY 10012, by arrangement with Houghton Mifflin Company. TRUMPET and the TRUMPET logo are registered trademarks of Scholastic Inc.

12 11 10 9 8 7 6 5 4 3 2 1   7 8 9/9 0 1 2/0

Printed in the U.S.A.

One day a little bunny woke up
from a long nap
alone under a tall elm tree. He heard
the silence of the woods around him
and wanted other rabbits like himself
for company.

"Can you tell me where I will find other rabbits?" he asked a sleepy old owl in the elm tree.

"Other rabbits?" said the owl, "Why there are always rabbits at Easter."

"Where is Easter?" asked the little bunny eagerly.

But the old owl had dozed off to sleep again in the bright sun.

"It must be some place to the East," thought the bunny and he set off searching.

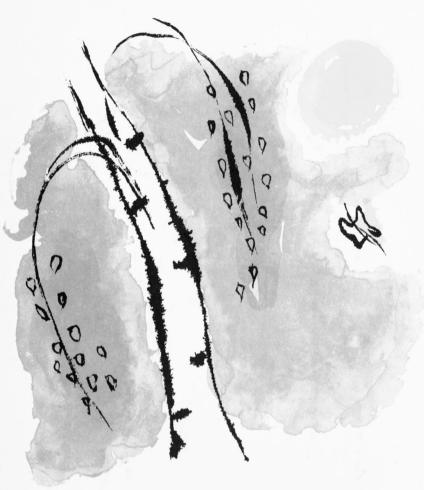

It was a hot summer day. The leaves

in the trees stood as still as a painting

against the blue sky. The bunny found

a pool of water, and down in the water
silvery trout flashed by. But there were
no bunnies about.

"Then this can't be Easter," he thought,
and went on his way.

He came to a field full of daisies.

There was a hot summer daisy smell over

the field and the bunny's nose twinkled.

A big slow bumble bee hummed by.

But in all that whiteness of daisies there

was no whiteness of bunnies like himself.

"This isn't Easter," the bunny said,

and he went on.

Once he was caught in a summer storm.
The sky looked like night. Suddenly
a streak of lightning, the color of stars,
forked through the sky. Great rumblings
rolled from one end of the world to the other.
The rain came down so fast that the
bunny could hardly see the mountain
laurel just ahead.

Slowly the rumbling rolled by.

Slowly the sky brightened.

Slowly the rain stopped.

He could see the mountain laurel with
wet shining leaves, each flower cup filled
with one sparkling drop of rain. But he
couldn't see any other bunnies shaking the
rain off their wet white fur.

"Not Easter," he said sadly,

and hurried on his way.

Summer was nearly over.

The leaves on the forest trees began to turn, brown and gold and red. Dead leaves crackled under the soft rabbit hops of the little bunny who was looking for Easter.

He stopped under a tree to rest and a round shiny red apple fell down and startled him. It smelled of autumn and crispness. He took a bite with his two front sharp teeth. When he had crunched the apple to its seeds, he looked around and sighed. There wasn't another bunny to be seen.

One day it began to snow. Soft white
flakes drifted down from the sky, and the
air was sharp and cold and still. When he
hopped through the white drifts he left
little dark footprints in the snow. But

no matter which way he hopped, his
footprints never crossed other bunny
footprints. The little bunny was alone in a
world without rabbits.

There were birds, little black sparrows like ink drops in the snow. Brown squirrels leaped about in the bare branches of the trees. Once he saw a whole family of deer slipping into the forest at dawn. But there wasn't another long eared, pink nosed, white furry rabbit like himself to be seen.

"This can't be Easter yet," he thought,

and his loneliness grew inside of him.

That night the bunny

curled up in a

hollow tree to keep

himself warm

out of the wind

and sharp air.

When he woke up next morning
there was something different.
It smelled . . . he quivered
his nose and smelled hard
. . . it smelled of wet growing
things. It smelled of
greenness and warm soft
sunlight. The little bunny
felt sure he would come
to Easter soon.

In the forest the black twigs
had little tight curled green buds.
The birds were singing high up
in the trees as the bunny
hopped ahead looking for Easter.

Suddenly he saw something in the muddy earth that made him stand perfectly still with excitement. Crossing in front of him, and going into the woods where he had never been, were little rabbit paw prints on the ground!

He followed the paw prints very carefully down a hidden path. There, in a clearing, he saw someone small and white resting on a mossy bank.

It was another bunny!

She had long ears like himself, and

eager bright eyes, like himself.

The little bunny was so happy to find her,

he completely forgot about Easter.

Hopping back through the forest with her, he showed her all the places he had seen on his search. At last they came to the tall elm tree where he had first awakened to find himself alone. But now his loneliness was gone. The two bunnies were very happy together.

Soon they had a whole family of little
rabbits, tiny, white sleepy things with
long sweet ears and small wet noses. The
bunny's heart throbbed with happiness
at this wonderful earthsmelling sunlit
bunny-filled world.

"Aha!" said the old owl when
he saw the bunny's family,
"didn't I tell you so? At Eastertime
there are always rabbits."

The bunny felt his little bunnies around him and the earth blooming beyond them, and all things growing. And he understood at last that Easter was not a *place* after all, but a *time* when everything lovely begins once again.